Moon Zoom

Turn the page to start the story.

The moon is
bright tonight.

The attic fills
with silver light.

Moon
Zoom

Written by Lesley Sims

Illustrated by David Semple

How this book works

The story of **Moon Zoom** has been written for
your child to read with your help. Encourage
your child to read as much as they can, helping
to sound out the words if they get stuck.

The moon is
bright tonight.

The attic fills
with silver light.

Jack
cannot sleep.

There are puzzles after the story, and for
these you will need to read the instructions to
your child.

You can find out more about helping your
child with this book, and with reading in
general, on pages 30-31.

Jack
cannot sleep.

"Ella!" he says.
"Let's go to the moon."

"Quick, pack a picnic.
Let's go soon!"

The rocket speeds
into the night.

The moon gets nearer...
Such a sight!

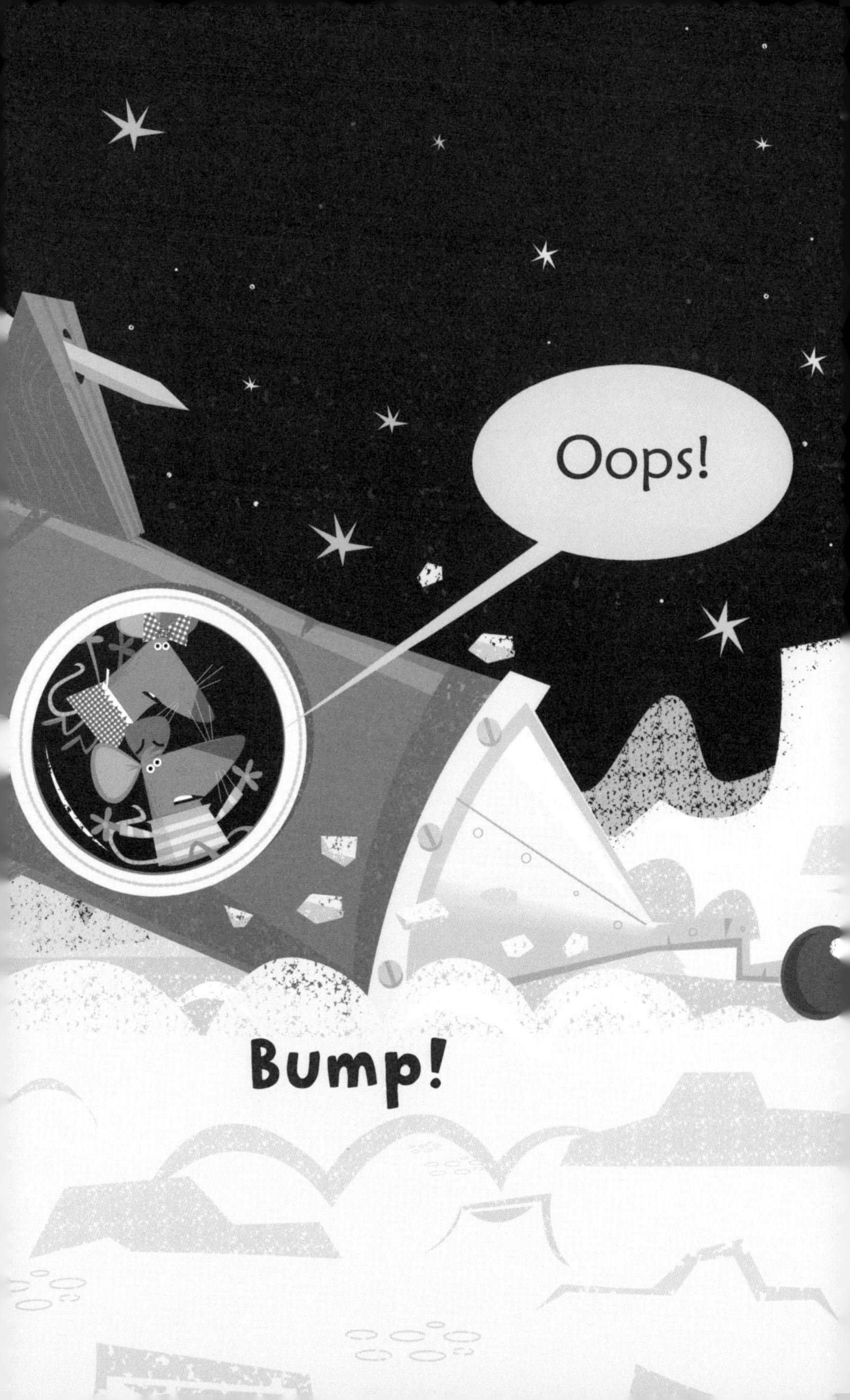
Oops!
Bump!

17

The picnic is laid
upon a rock.

Eek!

Ella jumps
in shock.

"Yes!" says Ella.
"Just wait for Jack."

"Jack?" she says...
Not a peep.

Now Jack is asleep!

Puzzle 1

Match the words to the pictures.

1. Now Jack is asleep!

2. "Oops!"

3. "Let's go to the moon."

4. "Let me unpack the picnic, dear."

5. The rocket speeds into the night.

A

B

C

D

E

Puzzle 2

There is one wrong word in the sentence below each picture. What should they say?

1.

Jack cannot creep.

2.

"We need a pocket."

3.

The spoon gets nearer.

4.

"Dust wait for Jack."

Puzzle 3

The words in each row should rhyme, but the last column is all mixed up. Can you put the words that rhyme together? The first one has been done as an example.

soon	noon	steep
night	light	rocket
bump	jump	moon
pocket	socket	flash
sleep	creep	bright
crash	splash	lump

Answers to puzzles

Puzzle 1

1. E Now Jack is asleep!

2. C "Oops!"

3. A "Let's go to the moon."

4. D "Let me unpack the picnic, dear."

5. B The rocket speeds into the night.

Puzzle 2

1. Jack cannot ~~creep.~~
   Jack cannot sleep.

2. "We need a ~~pocket.~~"
   "We need a rocket."

3. The ~~spoon~~ gets nearer.
   The moon gets nearer.

4. "~~Dust~~ wait for Jack."
   "Just wait for Jack."

Puzzle 3

soon	noon	moon
night	light	bright
bump	jump	lump
pocket	socket	rocket
sleep	creep	steep
crash	splash	flash

Guidance notes

Usborne Very First Reading is a series of books, specially developed for children who are learning to read. **Moon Zoom** is the eighth book in the series, and by this stage your child should be able to read the story alone, with occasional help from you.

In **Moon Zoom**, your child starts reading words that begin or end with two or more consonants, such as 'sleep', 'fills' or 'speeds'. The story also introduces simple two-syllable words, such as 'rocket' and 'picnic', and the letter-combination

er   as in **silver** or **better**

Learning to read patterns like these can more than double your child's reading vocabulary. Later books in the series introduce different ways of spelling sounds and pronouncing letters, while reinforcing the ones your child already knows.

You'll find lots more information about the structure of the series, advice on helping your child with reading, extra practice activities and games on the Very First Reading website,[*] **www.usborne.com/veryfirstreading**

[*]US readers go to **www.veryfirstreading.com**

Some questions and answers

- **Why do I need to read with my child?**
  Sharing stories makes reading an enjoyable and fun activity for children. It also helps them to develop confidence and stamina. Even if you are not taking an active part in reading, your listening and support are very important.

- **When is a good time to read?**
  Choose a time when you are both relaxed, but not too tired, and there are no distractions. Only read for as long as your child wants to – you can always try again another day.

- **What if my child gets stuck?**
  Don't simply read the problem word yourself, but prompt your child and try to find the right answer together. Similarly, if your child makes a mistake, go back and look at the word together. Don't forget to give plenty of praise and encouragement.

- **We've finished, now what do we do?**
  It's a good idea to read the story several times to give your child more practice and more confidence. Then, when your child is ready, you can go on to the next book in the series, **Run, Rabbit, Run!**

Edited by Jenny Tyler and Mairi Mackinnon
Designed by Russell Punter

First published in 2010 by Usborne Publishing Ltd., Usborne House,
83-85 Saffron Hill, London EC1N 8RT, England. www.usborne.com
Copyright © 2010 Usborne Publishing Ltd.